The Nutcracker's Night Before Christmas

Keith Brockett ★ *Illustrated by* Joseph Cowman

PUBLISHED *by* SLEEPING BEAR PRESS

'Twas the night before Christmas, and up in the town,
a theater stood high on a hill like a crown.
Its stately marquee glittered brightly with light
proclaiming *The Nutcracker*'s opening night.

But backstage the mood was uncertain and stressed.
Disasters had struck as the day had progressed.
And now, as the curtain time quickly drew near,
a sick sense of panic was growing severe.

The programs had come from the printer that day
with titles misspelled, *The Nutsnacker* Ballet.
The error was funny and might have amused,
if not for those programs that couldn't be used.

But far bigger problems had reared up their heads.
The stagehands got sick and went home to their beds.
The spotlights had fallen—the stage was left dim
and Clara spilled grape juice all over the scrim.

The grumpy old cat living under the stage
had clawed the tulle skirts into shreds in a rage.
The Snowflakes and Flowers were in total despair.
They couldn't perform without costumes to wear!

The sword for the Mouse King just couldn't be found.
The nutcracker smashed when it dropped to the ground.
The tutus had lost all their sequins and gems,
and scraps of torn stitching hung loose from their hems.

But worse was to come. With a crash! And a yell!
The Christmas tree used in the party scene fell!
Its ornaments shattered across the stage floor
and none of its lights would light up anymore.

With that, any hope for the show was now gone.
It had to be canceled. It couldn't go on.
The problems and mishaps were far past repair,
and sad disappointment hung stale in the air.

But then a surprising and strange thing occurred:
from one of the set pieces, noises were heard.
A fireplace stood onstage—set in a wall—
and from it came laughter that filled the whole hall!

The set began shaking, and then the stage too,
until old St. Nicholas burst from the flue!
He'd seen that the show was in trouble that night,
from far overhead on his Christmas Eve flight.

He called to his elves. They appeared from thin air!
And got right to work—there was no time to spare.
They fixed all the costumes, the spotlights, and tree,
then printed new programs as fast as could be.

They handled the hassles with props and the scrim,
and suddenly things were not looking so grim!
The elves took the places of sick stagehands too,
and changed all the lighting and sets right on cue.

And one more surprise was in store for that night:
the Sugarplum Fairy, that magical sprite—
she flew from the wings in a wondrous display,
for St. Nick had lent her his reindeer and sleigh!

She landed onstage to the thrill of the crowd!
A standing ovation was heard, long and loud.
The show had been saved, thanks to dear Santa Claus—
let's give him a rollicking round of applause!

The Nutcracker Ballet

The Nutcracker ballet is a wonderful story, full of magic and drama, told through the art of dance. The music plays, the dancers dance—no words are spoken throughout the entire performance.

The story of *The Nutcracker* goes like this: It's Christmas Eve, and Clara Silberhaus's parents are throwing their annual Christmas Eve ball. All their friends and family have been invited. Clara's Uncle Drosselmeyer, a talented toy maker, arrives at the party with four life-like mechanical dolls, who dance to the delight of all. He also has gifts for all the children, and to Clara, he gives a nutcracker: a wooden doll carved in the shape of a little man, used for cracking hazelnuts. Clara loves the present. But her brother Fritz becomes jealous of it; he snatches the nutcracker away from Clara and smashes it on the floor. Clara cries over the broken doll until her Uncle Drosselmeyer sees her plight and repairs it.

The ball continues late into the night. But eventually the party ends, and the guests depart. After everyone has gone to bed, Clara sneaks downstairs to retrieve her beloved nutcracker, which she left under the Christmas tree. But as she reaches for the doll, the clock strikes midnight, and to her amazement, she looks up to see her Uncle Drosselmeyer perched mysteriously atop the clock....

All at once, mice the size of men begin to fill the room! The Christmas tree grows to dizzying heights. The nutcracker also grows to life-size, as do an army of Fritz's toy soldiers. Clara finds herself in the midst of a battle between the toy soldiers led by her nutcracker and the mice led by an evil Mouse King. The Mouse King manages to wound the nutcracker. But just as he is about to kill him, Clara throws her slipper at the Mouse King.

This distracts the Mouse King just long enough for the nutcracker to turn and stab him. The Mouse King dies on the nutcracker's blade. All the mice retreat, carrying away their vanquished leader.

The nutcracker then transforms into a handsome prince and leads Clara through the moonlit night, through a magnificent pine forest in the Kingdom of Snow. The Snowflakes dance all around them beside their Snow King and Queen.

Eventually they emerge from the forest into the Nutcracker Prince's homeland, the beautiful Kingdom of Sweets ruled by the Sugarplum Fairy. The Prince tells the Fairy how Clara saved him from the Mouse King. And she is so grateful to Clara that she arranges a celebration of sweets from around the world to dance in her honor. Spanish Chocolate, Arabian Coffee, Chinese Tea, Russian Candy Canes, Marzipan Shepherdesses with their flutes, Mother Ginger and her children, and a beautiful bouquet of waltzing Flowers all perform for Clara's amusement. Finally, the Sugarplum Fairy and her Cavalier honor Clara with a dance. Then they crown Clara and the Nutcracker Prince as rulers of the Kingdom of Sweets.

Suddenly, Clara awakens in her parlor under the Christmas tree with her nutcracker doll tucked under her arm. Was it all just a dream? She finds her crown from the Sugarplum Fairy sitting beside her.... Maybe it wasn't a dream after all!

Glossary

applause: clapping the hands together to show enjoyment of a performance

backstage: the area of a stage that is out of sight of the audience, where performers prepare to go onstage and where sets for upcoming scenes are stored

cue: a signal that lets a performer or a stagehand know when to do something

marquee: the sign on the outside of a theater, above its main entrance, that lists the name of the show being performed

ovation: loud, enthusiastic applause; when the audience stands to give an ovation, it shows even greater appreciation for the performance

program: a paper or booklet given to audience members that tells who the performers are in a show, who wrote the show and its music, and who created the dances; for classical ballets and operas, it might also give an outline of the story to be performed onstage

prop: any movable object used by performers in a show that helps them tell the story; the Nutcracker doll and the Mouse King's sword are examples of props

scrim: a large sheet of thin fabric used as a backdrop onstage. It can look like a solid wall when lit from the front, but when lit from behind, the audience can see through it

set: the scenery, furniture, and other items on a stage that identify the location in which the scenes in a show take place, such as a ballroom, a forest, or a castle

spotlight: a lamp that shines a strong beam of light on a fixed area, used to focus attention on a stage performer

stagehand: a person who works backstage at a theater, setting up the stage, changing sets between scenes during the show, operating lights and the curtain, and helping performers with their costumes and props. A show can't go on without a good crew of stagehands

tulle: a thin, stiff, net-like fabric used to make tutus, skirts, veils, and gowns

tutu: a short, fluffy skirt worn by ballerinas

wings: part of the backstage; the areas to the right and left of a stage, out of sight of the audience, where performers prepare to go onstage

For my three beautiful nieces: Genesis, Noelani, & Halle
—Keith Brockett

For my Savannah, who loves dance and theater
—Joseph Cowman

Library of Congress Cataloging-in-Publication Data
Brockett, Keith. The Nutcracker's Night before Christmas / written by Keith Brockett ;
illustrated by Joseph Cowman.
pages cm
Summary: "In The Nutcracker's Night Before Christmas preparations for a
doomed stage production of the classic ballet goes from terribly bad to
ridiculously worse. But it's Christmas Eve and help is on the way!"--Provided by the publisher.
ISBN 978-1-58536-889-1
1. Ballet dancing--Juvenile poetry. 2. Tchaikovsky, Peter Ilich,
1840-1893. Shchelkunchik--Juvenile poetry. 3. Moore, Clement Clarke,
1779-1863. Night before Christmas--Juvenile poetry. I. Cowman, Joseph, illustrator. II. Title.
PS3602.R6252N88 2015
811'.6--dc23
2015001608

1 3 5 7 9 10 8 6 4 2

Printed in the United States.

Sleeping Bear Press™

2395 South Huron Parkway, Suite 200
Ann Arbor, MI 48104

© 2015 Sleeping Bear Press
Visit us at sleepingbearpress.com